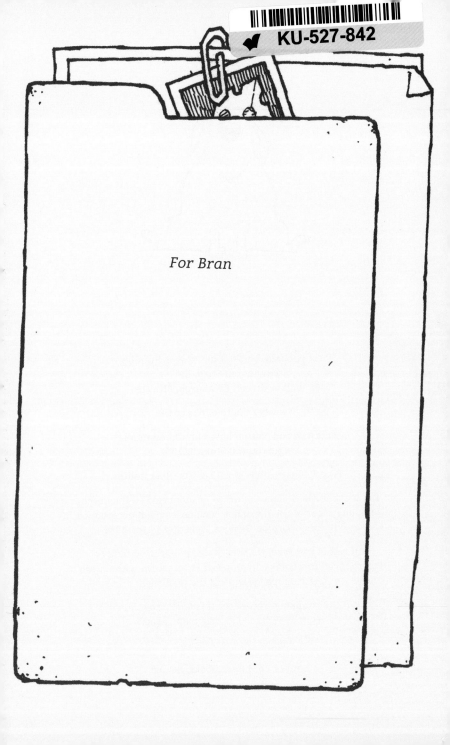

For Bran

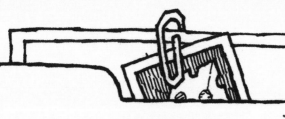

CONTENTS

Chapter 1
Aaaaaaah!

aah!"

Hal yelled.

Chapter 2
Another Cheesemare

"Was it another bad dream?" asked Hal's mum. "A nightmare?" asked Hal's dad with a yawn.

"No," said Hal. He picked up his pad and pencil. "It was another **cheesemare**."

"No more cheese before bed!" snapped Hal's dad. "This has got to stop!"

Hal knew his dad was right, but he wanted to find out if there really was a link between his cheesy snacks and the nightmares he was having every night.

Hal first spotted the link when he ate some smelly French cheese for supper and had a bad dream about vampires.

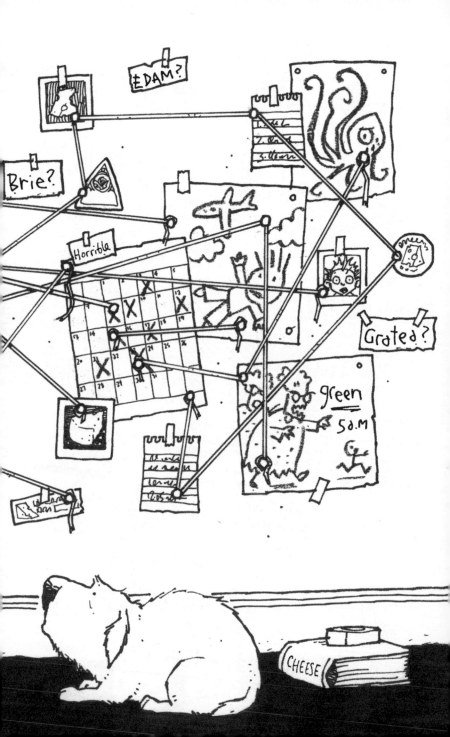

He began to try different cheeses to see what happened. Edam gave him nightmares of pork pies with teeth. Danish Blue cheese woke Hal with a start from a dream about great big green grannies. Cheddar made him dream of kittens with 16 eyes. With Gorgonzola it was farts that melted his skin. Hal tried to forget what he saw after a few small bits of Stilton.

Hal sat down with a thump in front of his Cheesemares Wall.

"This can't go on," he said to Rufus. **"Tomorrow I'm going to crack the Case of the Cheesemares once and for all."**

Chapter 3
Where to Start?

"Today I'm going to crack the Case of the Cheesemares once and for all," Hal said to his mum as he scoffed down his breakfast.

"That's nice, dear," said Hal's mum, and patted his head.

Hal packed some snacks, pulled on his boots and took a jumper. He packed the labels from all the different cheeses he'd tried and went downstairs.

His mum stood at the front door. She gave Hal his lunch box and Rufus's lead.

"Here's some lunch in case you get hungry,"
she said.

"And take Rufus. He's fat and needs more
walks."

Outside in the street, Hal didn't know
where to start. He took one of the labels he
had collected out of his backpack and looked
at it.

"Where to start ... where to start ...?" he
said to himself.

"Shop," growled Rufus.

"I know!" said Hal. "We'll start at the
cheese shop!"

Chapter 4
The Trail

Hal tied Rufus up outside the cheese shop. He took one last gulp of fresh air and went in. The smell inside the cheese shop was awful.

"Good morning, Mr Halloumi," said Hal.

"Good morning, Hal," smiled Mr Halloumi.

"What cheese do you want to try today, my friend?" asked Mr Halloumi as he picked some feta off his apron.

"No cheese today," said Hal. "I need to solve the Case of the Cheesemares."

He handed the labels from his backpack to Mr Halloumi. "All of these cheeses give me terrible nightmares and I want to find out why."

"Oh dear," said Mr Halloumi. "That's no good. Let me see."

He looked through the labels, then went off to the back shop.

After a while, Mr Halloumi came back.

"I'm sorry. I can't crack the Case of the Cheesemares for you, Hal," he said. "But I can tell you one thing – all these cheeses came from the same factory." He held out a form which said:

Contessa Von Udderstein's

(not-at-all-evil)

House of Cheese

Lovely Cheeses for the Kiddies

"This could be the lead I'm after," said
Hal as he undid Rufus's lead. "But where do
we go next?"

"Airport," said Rufus.

Chapter 5
Getting There

"Two tickets for Bovinia, please," said Hal to a lady at the airport.

"You're in luck," said the lady. "Flights to Bovinia are going cheap today! 60p for you, 70p for the dog."

"Why is Rufus's ticket more than mine?" asked Hal.

"Because he's fat and we'll have to hoover the seat after."

Rufus scowled at the lady.

The flight didn't take long at all. There were magazines, snacks and a film about a lobster that went into outer space.

Then they had to get a train. The train was very busy. There were magazines and snacks but no film.

19

Then Hal and Rufus had to get a bus. There were magazines but no snacks or film.

After that, Hal and Rufus went on by goat.
There were no magazines, snacks or film.

At last they arrived at:

Contessa Von Udderstein's
(not-at-all-evil)
House of Cheese.

Chapter 6
The House of Cheese

"Contessa von Udderstein's (not-at-all-evil) House of Cheese looks evil," said Hal.

It was true. Hal and Rufus hid behind some rocks and watched grubby trucks with dark windows drive in and out of the House of Cheese.

It was huge. Half-factory, half-castle. Three massive chimneys puffed muddy green smoke into the air above.

Now and then a bird flew too close to the smoke, choked and dropped like a stone from the sky. The smell was terrible – even worse than the smell of Mr Halloumi's shop.

"We need to get inside," said Hal. "We need to see what's going on."

Rufus didn't look too keen.

Hal and Rufus crept down the rocks to get closer to the House of Cheese. They hid from the trucks.

The trucks had to wait in a line to enter the factory. Hal and Rufus ran up to the last truck and jumped into the back. The old truck started up and they heard a buzzer screech. They were in the House of Cheese at last.

Hal and Rufus watched through a crack in the side of the truck.

When no one was looking, they jumped out.

"Let's head upstairs," hissed Hal. "We can see everything from up there."

Going upstairs may not have been the best idea. They could see everything, but the smell and fumes were terrible.

Rufus's poor doggy nose started to turn purple. Hal took a hanky from his pocket and poked it up Rufus's nostrils.

That helped with the smell, but the fumes were making Hal's eyes water with tears. He rubbed them and blinked down at the factory floor. What was down there? It looked like … it couldn't be … it looked like …

"**The House of Cheese is run by COWS!**" said Hal.

Chapter 7
Aaaachoooo!

Hal couldn't believe his eyes.

Hundreds of cows were busy down on the factory floor – some wore grubby white coats; others were in grubby overalls. They walked around on their back legs, looking after the ugly machines, packing the cheese and driving little forklift trucks around.

Hal turned to Rufus – was this just another bad dream? Rufus wasn't too bothered about the cows, but he didn't like the hanky up his nose.

His left nostril **twitched**.

Hal gasped.

His right nostril **itched**.

"No, Rufus! No!" hissed Hal.

His nose **wiggled** ...

jiggled ...

wriggled ...

and ...

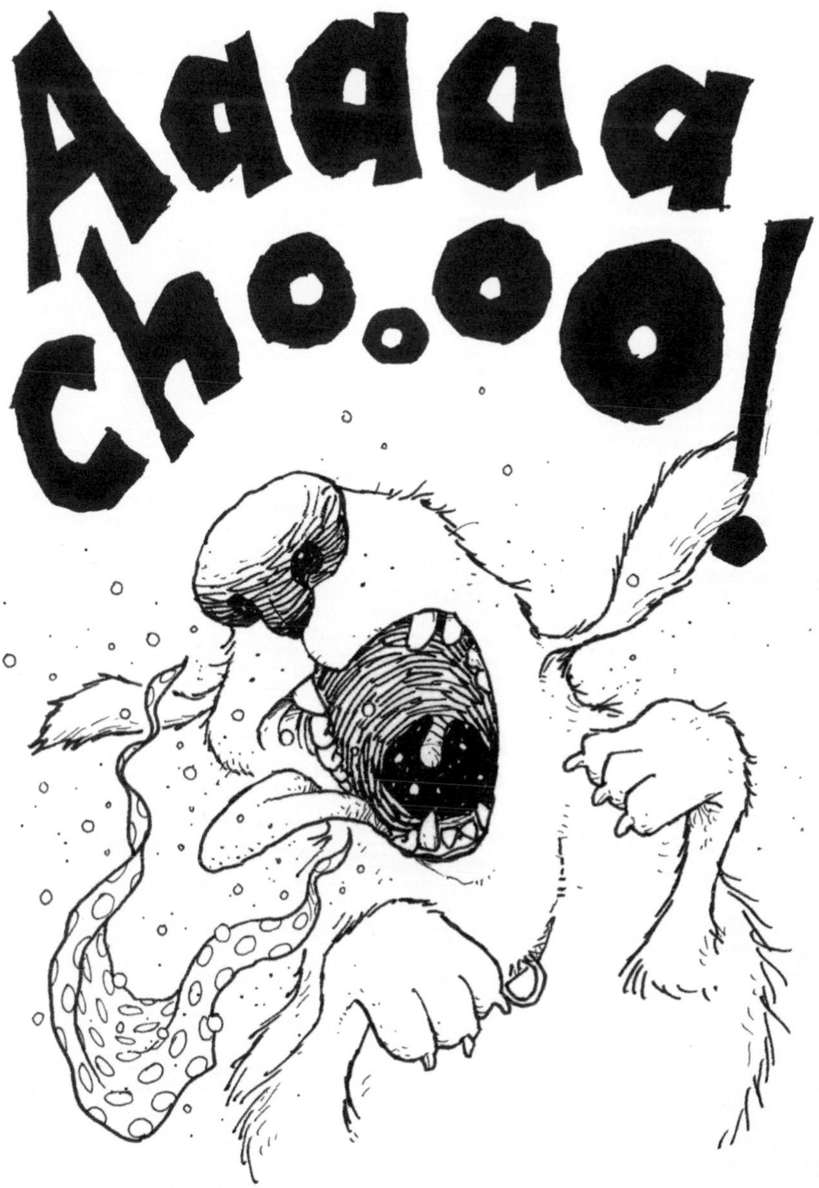
Aaaaa
choooo!

The busy factory went very very still ...
apart from the sound of hooves ... **getting
closer**.

In a moment the patrol cows were on them.

"**A HOOMAN!**" mooed one, and grabbed Hal.

"**AND A FAT DOG!**" mooed another, and
grabbed Rufus.

Rufus didn't like cows.

But there was no chance of escape.

"**Take them to ...**

CONTESSA VON UDDERSTEIN!"

Chapter 8
The Contessa

The cow patrol dragged Hal and Rufus down and down, deep into the House of Cheese. Every time Hal slowed down or stopped, one of the patrol cows pushed him in the back with a sharp hoof and shouted, "**MOOOOVE!**"

Soon they came to a grand door. One of the patrol cows rang the little cow bell that hung from the frame.

"Moo is it?" came a strange voice from inside.

"It's the patrol cows!" called the patrol cow.

"We've arrested a hooman and a fat dog!"

"Just a mooment!" called the voice. There was a sound of lady-like hoof-steps and then the voice bellowed, "**COME!**"

The patrol cows pushed Hal and Rufus into a room that was so grand it was like a palace. In the middle of the room stood the most evil cow in the world. **The Contessa von Udderstein.**

"So!" hissed the Contessa. "Hooman spies, is it? The last hoomans that sneaked in here were **cooked alive** in moolted cheese!"

Hal gulped. "You don't scare me, Contessa von Udderstein!" he yelled.

"Oh ... but I think I moo!" mocked the Contessa. "I scare millions of little hooman children like you **EVERY NIGHT** with my **CHEESEMARES!**"

"So it's true!" gasped Hal. "Your cheese does give children cheesemares! But why?"

"**Why? Why?!**" snapped the Contessa. "Like you don't know! **THEFT!** That's why! **Theft!** For years you nasty little hoomans have been **STEALING OUR MILK!** Stealing it with your little hooman fingers on your little hooman hands. **Stealing it!** And for what? To make milk shakes and yoghurt and ice cream and cheese and butter and sour cream and fudge and curds and whey and lassi and custard and ..."

"I get the picture," said Hal.

"**Yes!** I'm sure you moo!" snapped the Contessa. "And soon billions of children across the world will get the picture too! They'll get horrible pictures in their nasty little heads EVERY NIGHT! EVERYWHERE! We're going GLOBAL! Evil cheese made with our evil milk will soon be for sale all around the WORLD!"

The Contessa began to laugh. It was not a nice laugh.

It was a horrible evil cow laugh.

"Moo Hoo Ha! MOO! HOO HOO HA!"

Rufus didn't like evil cow laughter. It was even worse than a hanky up his nose.

"Run," he said.

"What?" said Hal.

"**Run!**" barked Rufus. He jumped up and bit
Contessa von Udderstein right on the udder.

Chapter 9
Run!

Have you ever heard the scream of an evil cow when a fat dog has bitten her udder? It is the worst sound in the world.

Contessa von Udderstein went mad. She kicked and shook and tried her hardest to throw off Rufus as evil milk from her udders spurted all over the room.

The patrol cows ran to and fro, grabbing at Rufus as he swung around and around. None of them could catch him. Their hooves couldn't hold on to his flying fur.

Hal watched in shock for a moment, then he remembered what Rufus had barked at him and he began to run!

Hal fled up and down many corridors until
at last he got to the big hall in the middle
of the factory. Alarm bells began to ring all
around the House of Cheese. Red lights flashed
on the walls and lit up the machines.

Hal could hear hooves hammer the factory
floor as the cows spread out to track him
down.

It wasn't long before they found him.

"**Here's the hooman!**" one cow shouted.

"**Get it!**" mooed another.

Hal was smaller and faster than the cows, but there were lots of them. He decided to head up the way. He hoped the cows weren't good climbers.

Hal jumped up onto a huge mixing machine and began to climb.

But the cows followed him. They were fast and they were getting closer.

Hal jumped from one machine to another. Still the cows followed.

They were getting closer.

Hal ran along the top of a mixing machine, grabbed a long tube and swung across to an enormous tank.

There was a ladder on the side of the tank, and Hal began to climb. He looked down. The cows weren't very good at swinging, but he knew they would get across and catch him soon.

Hal climbed on, higher and higher until he reached the top of the tank. He looked down and saw the cows on their way up. He looked back. More cows were coming up the ladder. **He was trapped!**

Hal sat down on the top of the tank. There was a flap open next to him and he saw evil green milk churning around inside the tank. It swirled and splashed and smelled like death.

Hal looked in his backpack. Did he have anything that could help him escape?

A sandwich? No.

A biscuit? No.

Goat Farming Today magazine? No.

A carton of Happy Dairies Pure Milk? ...

What would happen, thought Hal, to an **evil milk machine** if he poured in some Happy Dairies **pure milk**?

There was only one way to find out. Hal popped off the cap and poured the clean white milk into the churning green below.

For a moment nothing happened.

Then there was a **creak**.

Then a **deep groan** inside the tank.

The cows stopped climbing.

A small puff of steam hissed out.

Then the **bangs** started and the **clunks** and the **clanks**.

The cows ran.

They didn't care about Hal any more. They just ran for it – some on two legs, some on four for even more speed.

Hal thought running was a good idea.

He slid down the side of the tank and ran as fast as he could out of the factory.

He ran like the wind out of the House of
Cheese. He ran fast, but not as fast as Rufus,
who was suddenly there right next to him, with
the end of a cow tail in his mouth.

They had just got away when they turned
to see ...

Chapter 10
Getting Back

61

Chapter 11
Case Closed

Hal and Rufus made it home just in time for tea.

"Well?" asked Hal's mum. "Did you solve the Case of the Cheesemares once and for all?"

"Yes, thank you," said Hal.

"That's nice," said Hal's mum. "You're just in time for dinner. Go and wash your hands."

"You're in luck, son," smiled Hal's dad. "It's your favourite. Macaroni cheese."